The Adventures of Scuba Jack
Copyright 2023 by Beth Costanzo

A

Scuba Jack was sunning himself on the dock
attached to his houseboat.
There was a very large aquarium next to him
with an unusually smart octopus living within.

The very smart octopus would fan Scuba Jack when he was hot.
He would give him a high five each morning before they would begin their day.
He would also pass him a glass of lemonade when it was hot.
They were the best of friends.

The octopus loved living in the aquarium because all the creatures in the tank were also his friends.

There was an orange snail,
A red crab,

A Blue Tang,
A green Parrot Fish,

A white Angel Fish,
A brown Lionfish,

A yellow Butterfly Fish,
And a purple Triggerfish.

Scuba Jack didn't know it, but the octopus would escape daily.
He would jump into the sea and visit his family and friends.

Scuba Jack sat on the deck gazing at the stars.
He heard a splash and looked over at the aquarium
and noticed a very peculiar site.

He saw his friend the octopus. Next to his friend the octopus, was another octopus, and two baby octopuses peering at him.

"What in the world! You have a family? How did you all get in there?"

Scuba Jack was so excited to see his friend the Octopus with his family. Scuba Jack knew the most important thing in the world is family and love.

Being a family means that you are part of something special. All the creatures of the sea were Scuba Jack's family, and this made him happy.

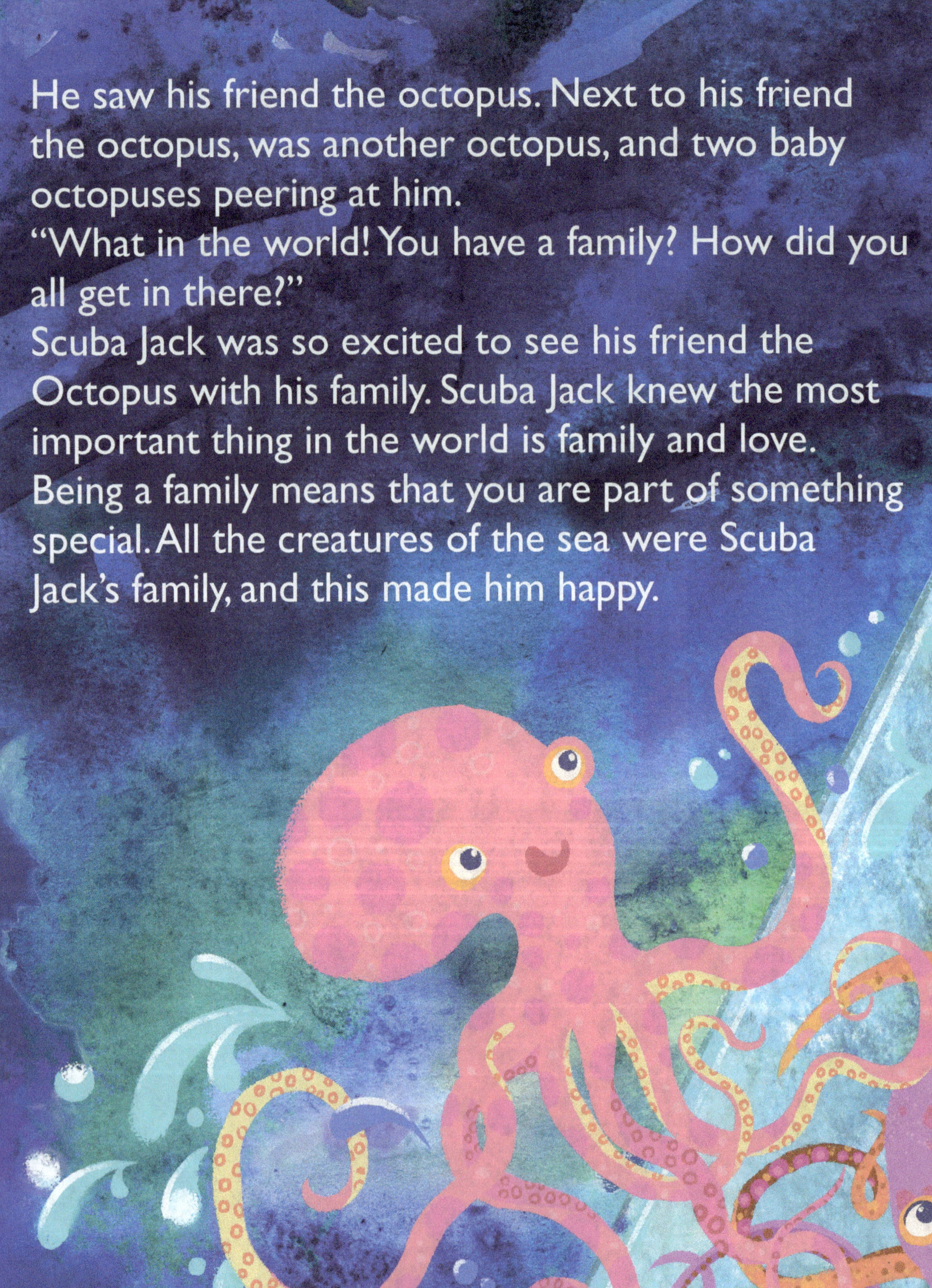

Suddenly two dolphins squirted water at Scuba Jack
to get his attention. A colorful ball went back and
forth between the dolphins.

Scuba Jack jumped into the water to play
with his friends yelling, "CANNONBALL!"
The sun began to set on Scuba Jack's home.
It was a TERRIFIC day!